# Sky & Sea

For the kids close by: Andrew and Allie,
who inspired us from the start, Mark, Kelsey,
Henning and Anna, for your love, encouragement
and fine outlook on life! With love.
—M.C. & C.C.


I dedicate this book to God and to my
wonderful wife Melissa. You inspire me with
your physical and spiritual beauty.
—T.K.

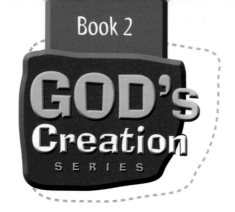

Book 2

# GOD's Creation
### SERIES

# Sky & Sea

Written & Illustrated by

Michael & Caroline Carroll

Cartoons by Travis King

zonderkidz

www.zonderkidz.com

*Book 2: Sky & Sea*
Text and illustration copyright © 2005 by Michael and Caroline Carroll
Cartoons copyright © 2005 Travis King
Rainbow photo on page 11 courtesy John Day.
Sun halo photo on page 12 courtesy Dennis Mammana.
Aurora photo on page 16 courtesy Dennis Mammana.
Space Shuttle Aurora photo on page 17 NASA/JSC.
Hurricane photo on page 25 courtesy National Aeronautics and Space Administration,
    Johnson Space Flight Center.

Requests for information should be addressed to:
Zonderkidz, Grand Rapids, Michigan 49530

**Library of Congress Cataloging-in-Publication Data**

Carroll, Michael W., 1955-
   Sky & sea / written and illustrated by Michael and Caroline Carroll.– 1st ed.
       p. cm. – (God's creation series ; bk. 2)
   ISBN 0-310-70579-7 (softcover)
   1.  Creation–Juvenile literature. 2.  Nature–Religious aspects–Christianity–Juvenile literature.
[1. Creation. 2. Nature–Religious aspects–Christianity. 3. Weather–Religious aspects–
Christianity.] I. Title: Sky and sea. II. Carroll, Caroline, 1956- III. Title.
   BS651.C3348 2005
   231.7'65–dc22

                                                              2003026699

*Editor: Barbara Scott*
*Art direction & design: Laura Maitner-Mason*
*Production artist: Sarah Jongsma*
*Cover design: Chris Tobias*
*Scientific review:  Larry Green, Denver meteorologist*
*Theological review: Dr. Stanley R. Allaby*

Printed in China
05 06 07 08 09/CTC/5 4 3 2 1

*A Special Word About*

# God's Creation Series

God created the heavens and the earth, and lots of other cool stuff too! We divided our books up in a way that is like the creation week described in Genesis, but we put a few things in different places so that we can understand them better. In Book One we talk about the beginning of the universe along with the stars and planets, while the Bible talks about the sun, moon, and stars on the fourth day. Don't worry—we noticed! God's Creation Series is about the wonders of God's creation, and not so much about when each event took place. So hold on for the ride of your life—through time and space—to enjoy the great things made by our great God!

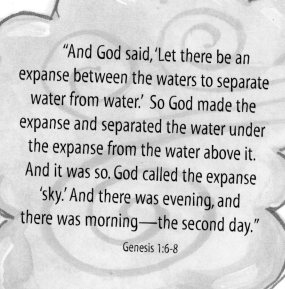

"And God said, 'Let there be an expanse between the waters to separate water from water.' So God made the expanse and separated the water under the expanse from the water above it. And it was so. God called the expanse 'sky.' And there was evening, and there was morning—the second day."

Genesis 1:6-8

# How about a dip?

It's easy to get wet if you live on Earth. Oceans surround us. Vast oceans of water slosh across the face of our world. A great ocean of air swirls above and around us. In the beginning of creation, you couldn't tell where one ocean stopped and the other started. The atmosphere was full of water vapor (microscopic water drops).

Then God separated "water from water." When God separated the waters from the sky, really cool stuff started to happen. God separated water into the waters above (clouds, snow, and rain) and the waters below (oceans, rivers, and lakes). First, let's take a look at all the awesome things God put in the sky. From there, we'll travel to the waters below and see how air and water work together.

WATER EVERYWHERE! OUR PLANET TODAY HAS 326 MILLION CUBIC MILES OF WATER. OF THAT AMOUNT, 3,100 CUBIC MILES ARE UP IN THE AIR!

## The Waters Above: Heads Up!

The sky looks like an empty bowl, but actually, it's full of wonderful stuff. There's a lot of water up there. The sky's full of air, too. It's full of swirling storms, crashing lightning, and glowing rainbows. It's full of clouds. Look up! What do you see? If it's a sunny day, you'll see a whole lot of blue.

Have you ever wondered why the sky is blue? Air has no color, but sunlight does. In fact, the light from the sun has all the colors of the rainbow. As the waves of light shine through all the molecules of air, the short wavelengths of light (which are blue) get through more easily than the longer wavelengths (which are red and keep running into those pesky molecules). At sunset and sunrise, most of the blue light is scattered away by the time it gets to us, leaving only the faint red and yellow light.

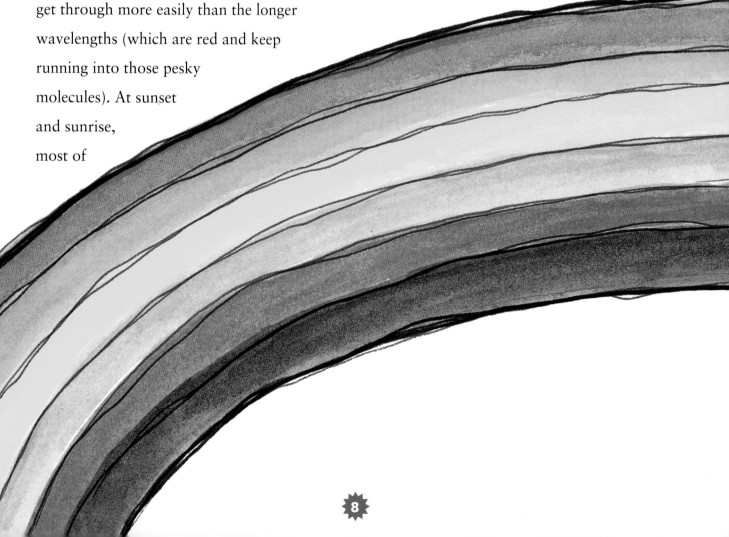

God placed many things in the sky to be signs to people. We have seen the sun, moon, and stars already in *Book One* of God's Creation Series. God said, "Let there be lights in the expanse of the sky to separate the day from the night, and let them serve as signs to mark seasons and days and years" (Genesis 1:14).

Take a look into a distant thunderstorm and you'll see another wonderful sign God has placed in the sky—the rainbow. Every single color in the sunlight can be seen in a rainbow. Why? Sunlight reflects off each raindrop, so it gets split into all of its colors. All this sunlight bouncing around forms a graceful arc of color across the sky, going from red on the outside, to orange, yellow, green, blue, indigo, and violet. It's God's original tie-dye!

# Crazy Colors

A rainbow is actually a full circle. We can only see part of it because the ground gets in the way. Rainbows appear exactly opposite the sun, so we mostly see them in early morning and late afternoon, when the sun is low.

The Bible tells us the story of Noah and a great flood in Genesis 6:9—9:17. The people of the earth had become mean and wicked, except for Noah and his family. So God told Noah to build an ark (a big boat) to save himself, his family, and all the different kinds of animals on the earth. The Bible says God would make it rain for 40 days and 40 nights (Genesis 7:4). Talk about soggy socks!

Noah's neighbors made fun of him when he started to build the boat. Why? Had it never rained before? We don't know. Perhaps it seldom rained in that part of the world. What we know for sure is that this time, it rained so much the whole earth was covered in water. Not only did rain fall from the sky, but water burst from under the earth.

After the flood, God told Noah and his family that they should always remember his promises when they saw the rainbow. God said, "This is the sign of the covenant I am making between me and you and every living creature with you, a covenant for all generations to come…Never again will the waters become a flood to destroy all life" (Genesis 9:12,15).

God is a God of promises. The Bible says God never forgets, he always loves, and he never breaks a promise. When you see a rainbow, remember God's special promises to you, his child (and be thankful you have dry socks). Can you think of any other promises in the Bible?

*A beautiful rainbow reminds us of God's promises to us.*

When the air gets really chilly, water droplets freeze into ice crystals. These mini ice cubes split sunlight in the same way that raindrops do, but they're a different shape. Instead of being round like a blob of water, ice crystals are the shape of unsharpened pencils.

Sunlight coming through the ice crystals can be seen around the sun instead of on the other side of the sky. The bent light makes a big glowing circle called a halo. Halos have the same colors as rainbows with red inside and purple outside.

Sometimes, patches of ice crystals form part of a halo. Often, the parts of the halo are on either side of the sun, looking like little diamonds of rainbow colors. These diamonds are called sun dogs, because they follow the sun around like puppies.

Halos also circle the moon at night and are good predictors of a coming storm.

## The Air

If our atmosphere had a motto, it would be "to protect and serve." God has wrapped our Earth with a wonderful blanket of air to keep us from getting too warm or too cold, to protect us from radiation from space, and to give us something to breathe.

Out in space, there are lots of leftovers from the creation of the solar system. Space rocks—like meteors, asteroids, and comets—whiz around, often slamming into planets and moons. We know this from the craters we see on almost every surface in our solar system. The planets that have few craters usually have atmospheres to protect them.

How could something as thin as air keep meteors from hitting the ground? The answer, my friends, is friction. As a space rock falls toward the earth, it speeds up to about 36,000 miles per hour!

Meteors scream through our atmosphere, and tiny molecules of air bump into them, causing friction. Just as rubbing your hands together makes them warm, rubbing a rock against air—a whole lot of air—makes the rock warm too. And after awhile, the rock is so hot that it burns up. Many space rocks burn up in the atmosphere, and at night you can see them as shooting stars, streaks of light in the sky.

Of course, Earth is not standing still either. While spinning on its axis, Earth is also rotating around the sun. At the same time, our entire solar system is speeding

through space. So do meteors run into the earth, or does the earth run into all that leftover debris? A little of both! Where are the cosmic cops when you need them?

About 3,000 tons of space rocks rain down on Earth every day, mostly as dust. A few really big ones make it to the ground, blasting out craters. Thank God for our blanket of air! Without it, the forecast would be "partly scattered rock showers."

As the solar wind hits the earth's magnetic "shield," it makes curtains of light in the sky.

Our magnetosphere also protects us. This is visible on some dark nights, especially in the far northern and southern places of the globe. Curtains and banners of light dance across the sky. Sometimes the colors are faint gray and green, but they often flare into orange, yellow, and white. It's not a rainbow. It's not a halo. It's called the aurora borealis—also called the "northern lights" in the northern hemisphere, or the aurora australis—the "southern lights" in the southern hemisphere.

Auroras show us another way that God has protected our planet from the dangers of space. The sun is constantly spewing out a stream of deadly particles called "solar wind." But the earth has a blanket even higher than the air, and that blanket comes all the way from the core of the earth.

Inside the earth is molten rock, which acts like a gigantic magnet. It generates magnetic fields called the magnetosphere and forms a gigantic magnetic bubble around the earth. When solar wind blasts into this magnetic shield, most of it is stopped. But the few particles that make it through hit the gas in our next blanket—the atmosphere. As the particles crash into atoms of gas, the aurora forms. God gave us the magnetosphere and the atmosphere to protect us.

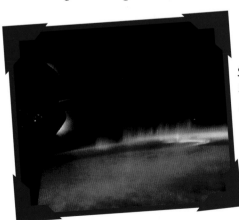

*Space Shuttle Aurora: In 1992 the Space Shuttle Atlantis used a special pair of electron guns to make the first man-made auroras. Scientists were able to explore how auroras form and develop using this experiment.*

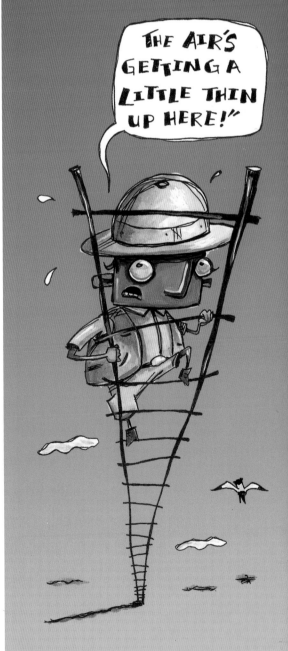

# Into Thin Air!

The air around the earth is thick near the ground, but it gets thinner the higher up you go. It disappears about 80 miles above us, and that's where space starts!

THE AIR'S GETTING A LITTLE THIN UP HERE!"

## Clouds

As the sun beats down on puddles, lakes, and oceans, some of the water floats up as water vapor. Water vapor is made up of molecules of water. They're so small that we can't see them. But high in the sky, the molecules cool off and slow down, sticking to each other and to tiny particles of dust. As more of the vapor clings together, it finally becomes a drop of water. If there are enough of these drops floating together, they become big enough for us to see. They become clouds.

Clouds are vapor. They are God's design for holding water up in the air until it comes down as rain, hail, sleet, or snow. Besides being handy storage tanks for moisture, clouds are beautiful. Next time you look at a cloud, notice how it changes as it travels across the sky and appreciate God's craftsmanship. He makes containers that change shape. Clouds are also nature's umbrellas, giving us shade from the hot sun.

High clouds are much colder than ones near the ground. In the middle of a summer afternoon, high above your head, there just may be a fierce snowstorm! But if the snow gets heavy enough to fall to the ground, it will melt on the way down and turn into a summer rain shower.

Clouds close to the ground are called stratus clouds.

Stratus clouds are fairly flat and thin. One of the most unusual types of stratus is called lenticular. Lenticular clouds form in air that rises over a mountain or high plain. They form a shape like a Frisbee, and indicate strong winds.

Higher, fluffy, cotton-ball clouds are called cumulus clouds. They look like piles of marshmallows. Above the cumulus clouds, altocumulus clouds look more ragged and disorganized.

GREAT BALLS OF ICE! THE LARGEST HAILSTONE EVER RECORDED FELL IN COFFEEVILLE, KANSAS. IT WAS AS BIG AS A HEAD OF CABBAGE!

CABBAGE

Anvil (Top of Cumulonimbus)

Cirrus

Cirrocumulus

Altostratus

Altocumulus

Cumulus

Cumulonimbus

Lenticular

Stratus

# Humidity

The amount of invisible water vapor in the air is called humidity. When humidity is low, the air is dry. When the air contains one hundred percent humidity, it's holding as much water as it can without raining.

Soggy Fact: We feel hotter when it's humid, because our bodies get rid of heat by sweating. The water on our skin evaporates and makes us cool. But when there is a lot of water in the air, the water on our skin can't evaporate as easily, so it's harder to chill out.

Try this. Ride your bike as fast as you can until you start to sweat. Now coast. If the humidity is lower, the air movement will help evaporate the moisture on your skin, and you will feel cooler.

Far up in the sky, seven or more miles, we see the thin wisps of cirrocumulus and cirrus clouds. Thin, graceful, wispy cirrus clouds float higher than a jet airliner flies. Cirrus clouds often catch the bright colors of sunset or sunrise because they are so high. When cirrus clouds appear, it often means that a storm is coming. There is a famous saying that comes from this fact: "Red sky at morning, sailors take warning."

Cumulonimbus clouds are the biggest, sometimes towering eleven miles up into the sky. We often call these clouds "thunderheads." A cumulonimbus cloud develops a flat top called an anvil. Thunderstorms, hail, and tornadoes come from this type of cloud.

As air moves around, it piles up in some places and thins out in others. Thinner air has low pressure. Low pressure is usually warmer and is a hint that a change in the weather is coming. A high-pressure system is usually cold and a sign of good weather. Watch out when the two systems crash together! More on that later.

ON AN AVERAGE DAY IN THE UNITED STATES, 40 TRILLION GALLONS OF WATER FLOAT ABOVE US IN THE SKY. ABOUT ONE TENTH OF THIS WATER FALLS DOWN AS SNOW, RAIN, OR HAIL EVERY DAY.

Water droplets and ice crystals rise and fall within cumulonimbus clouds. As they do, they build up static electricity, just like you do when you shuffle your feet on the carpet and then touch metal. But the little spark that zaps your finger is nothing compared to the flashing bolt of lightning in a cumulonimbus cloud.

Thunder, which is caused by lightning, can be loud and dramatic. Why would a bunch of electricity make so much noise? As a lightning bolt sizzles through the sky, the air around it heats up to 50,000 degrees. Ouch! But in a fraction of a second, the lightning is gone. The air expanded when it was super-heated, but now it chills out quickly. As the air crashes back in on itself, it makes a loud noise. That's thunder!

*Kaboom!* Light travels faster than sound, right? When you see lightning, the thunder is on its way to you, but it takes longer. For every five seconds between the lightning and thunder, the lightning is a mile away. If there's ten seconds between the flash and the boom, the lightning is two miles away.

*Many forest fires begin when lightning strikes dry trees.*

# Flash!

There are thousands of lightning storms all over the world right now. Lightning strikes the earth a hundred times every second!

Lightning bursts out of the clouds, but it also comes up from the ground. In a split second, there may be a dozen lightning bolts flashing back and forth from a cloud to the ground, all in the same path. It happens so fast that our eyes see only a flicker.

## The Water Cycle

When the sky cleared and the oceans formed, God did a very clever thing—he started the water cycle. The water cycle is described in Isaiah (55:10), Job (36:27), and other places in the Bible. The rain and snow fall from the sky, pools into lakes, and runs, as rivers, down to the oceans. Then water evaporates out of the ocean and returns to the sky. This drizzling merry-go-round is part of God's intricate design.

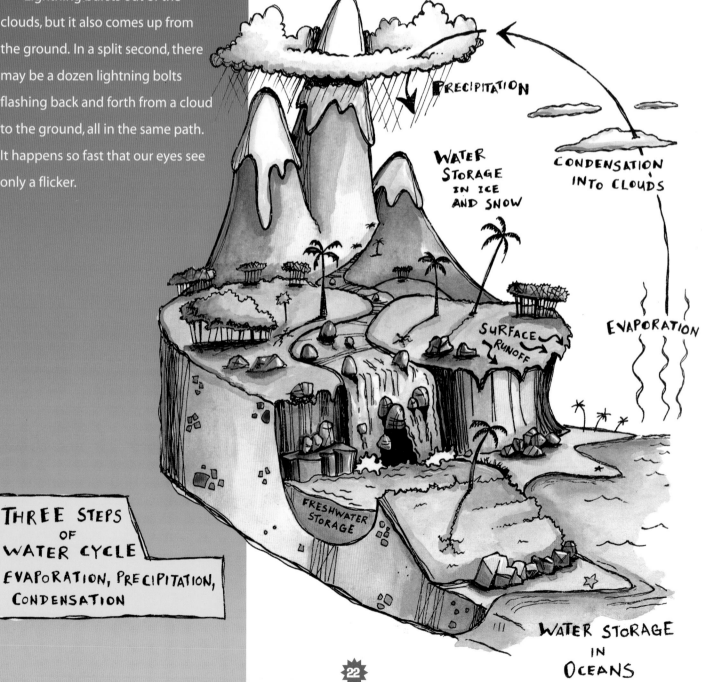

PRECIPITATION

WATER STORAGE IN ICE AND SNOW

CONDENSATION INTO CLOUDS

SURFACE RUNOFF

EVAPORATION

FRESHWATER STORAGE

THREE STEPS OF WATER CYCLE
EVAPORATION, PRECIPITATION, CONDENSATION

WATER STORAGE IN OCEANS

## Wind and Storms

The Spirit of God is like the wind. We cannot see him, but we can see the work he does in our friends, in our families, and even in us! The Spirit moves and blows where he will.

Like the Spirit of God, the world's air is in constant motion. As the earth turns in space, the air is pulled around with it. But the sun's heat mixes things up a bit. The air is heated over the equator—the middle of the earth. Air rises on both sides of the equator in great arcs of wind that move toward the top and bottom of the planet (where it's cooler).

In between these belts of wind are calm places called the doldrums. In ancient times, sailing ships became trapped for weeks at a time in the doldrums, until they drifted north or south and caught the wind currents again. The wind currents are like conveyor belts wrapped all the way around the earth.

The hottest places on Earth are not on the equator, but a little above and below

Jesus said, "The wind blows wherever it pleases. You hear its sound, but you cannot tell where it comes from or where it is going. So it is with everyone born of the Spirit."

John 3:8

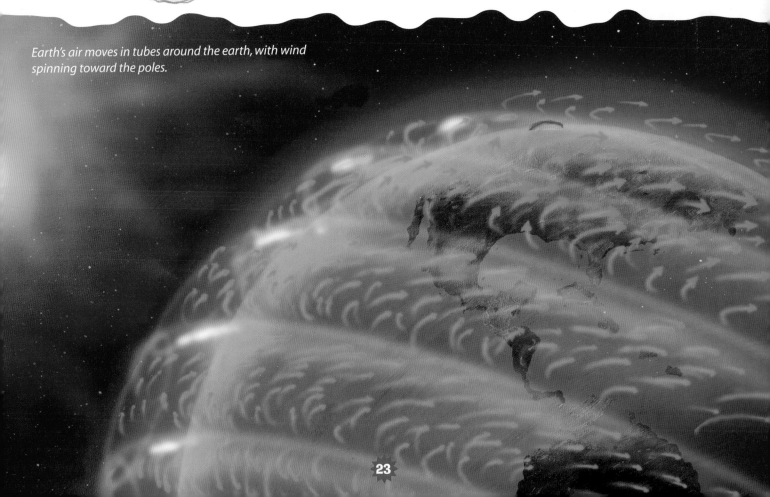

Earth's air moves in tubes around the earth, with wind spinning toward the poles.

# How to Make Weather

The sun beats down near the equator, heating up the air. Air over the poles (top and bottom) of the earth is cold. Hot and cold air is constantly moving around. Where hot meets cold, clouds form and weather happens! When warm air hits cold air, it forms a weather front. If you see a line of clouds in the sky, it could be a weather front.

it. This is because the world is tilted, so that sometimes the top half (or hemisphere) is tipped toward the sun, and sometimes the bottom hemisphere is. This means that most sunlight falls above and below the equator in bands called the horse latitudes. Here, skies are clear most of the time, and the winds are calm, very much like the doldrums. Most of the world's great deserts fall within these two bands, as we will see in Book Three of God's Creation Series.

At first, there were no mountains, valleys, and forests. But today, the air has currents that cycle fresh air from the forests into calm places on Earth. The rain forests drive air currents, as do the oceans and deserts. Mountains make the air flow in different directions, too. This is where high- and low-pressure systems (hot and cold air) come into play.

Winds can do some strange things. They can be fierce or gentle. They can bring a cool breath of air to a hot summer day. They can blow leaves off the trees or roofs off buildings.

Winds become strongest when they swirl into great pinwheel storms called hurricanes. Hurricanes are the most powerful storms on Earth. They are born over the ocean near the equator, where the air has been heating and soaking up water. The ocean has been storing heat for weeks or months, causing the air above it to circulate counterclockwise in the Northern Hemisphere and in the opposite direction south of the equator.

As the baby storm drifts to the north or south, its warm air begins to circle around cooler air. Around and around it goes, until its winds scream along as fast as one hundred eighty miles per hour. Grown-up hurricanes can

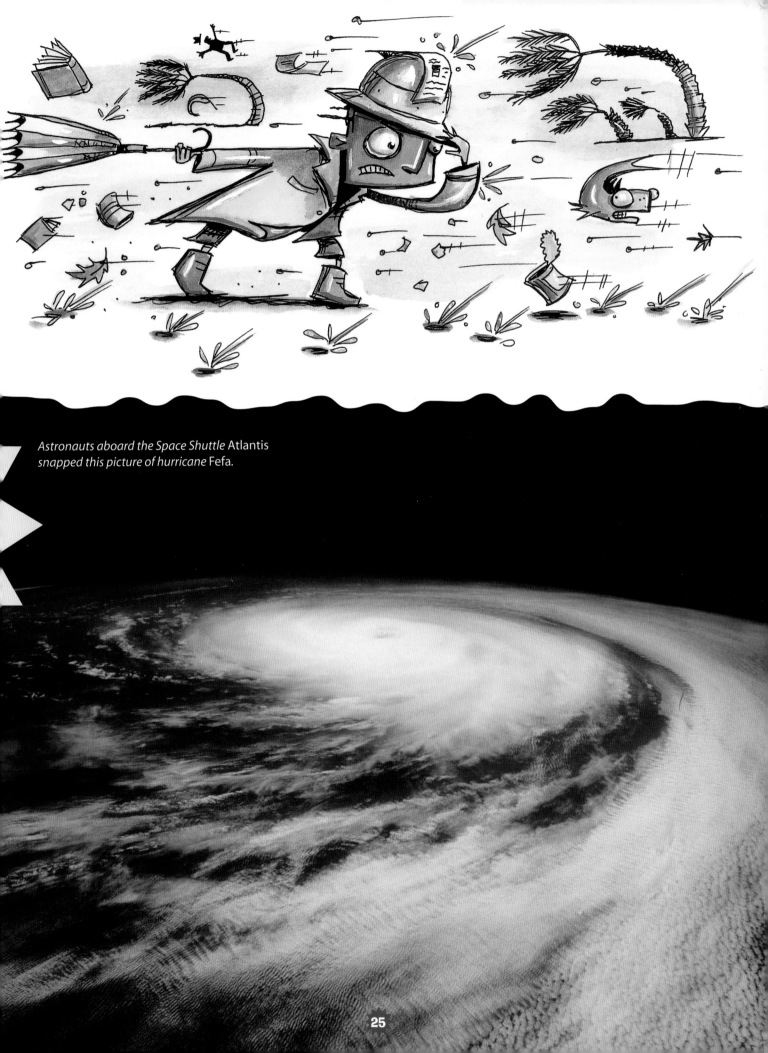

Astronauts aboard the Space Shuttle Atlantis snapped this picture of hurricane Fefa.

stretch across hundreds of miles of ocean. They trigger dangerous hailstorms and tornadoes.

Tornadoes are funnel-shaped tubes of spinning wind that can drop to the ground out of cumulonimbus clouds. They form when warm air rises and meets cold air up above. The two don't get along very well and swirl around each other in a powerful and deadly dance.

Cumulonimbus clouds produce thunderstorms, hail, and tornadoes. When a dry cold front moves east, thunderstorms develop

where it meets warm, moist air. These thunderstorms can produce tornadoes.

Tornadoes usually happen in the early spring and summer when strong fronts move through the middle of the United States, east of the Rocky Mountains. This area called "tornado alley" stretches from Texas to the Dakotas.

Tornadoes are called "weak" (rotating winds of 110 miles per hour or less), "strong" (rotating winds between 110 and 200 miles per hour), and "violent" (over 200 miles per hour). Violent

"CHECK THIS OUT! AN AVERAGE OF 936 TORNADOES HIT THE UNITED STATES EVERY YEAR!"

tornadoes are capable of picking up large trucks and flattening entire city blocks.

Really strange things can happen when a tornado hits an area. Tornadoes have been known to drive a piece of hay through a board, and at the same time lift a dog high into the sky and gently put it down again.

In the beginning of creation, the earth had no dry land, but there may have been tornadoes over the ocean. These are called waterspouts. Waterspouts are not usually as powerful as tornadoes, but they can still ruin the day for people out in boats!

His way is in the whirlwind and the storm, and clouds are the dust of his feet.

Nahum 1:3

## Climate

The weather changes every day just like you change your clothes (we hope), but over a number of years, the weather begins to average out. The pattern of weather that a place has over a long period of time is called climate. Tropical climates are at the equator where the rain forests grow. There, it rains a lot and is very hot. An area that has cold weather all the time is called arctic or alpine. Sun, sandstorms, and scorpions are found in desert climates.

# Names of Winds

Some winds are so predictable that they've been given names. The chinook is a warm wind that comes down from the Rocky Mountains to the plains. Monsoon winds bring rain and flooding to Asia. The simoom, or "poison wind," is a desert wind that brings violent dust storms, and the mistral blows cold mountain air through the valleys of France.

IN AUSTRALIA HURRICANES ARE CALLED WILLY-WILLIES.

# Goldilocks Climates

As we saw with our "just right" universe in Book One, God has made the earth just right for our climate and life. Our planet balances between too hot and too cold. If the earth were just a few degrees cooler, more ice and snow would cover the ground. Since ice and snow are white, they would reflect more sunlight off the ground, and it would get even colder, so more snow and ice would fall.

But if the earth were just a few degrees warmer, more of our water would be vapor up in the air (instead of liquid on the ground). This water vapor would hold in heat, so the earth would become warmer, and more water would turn to vapor. You get the picture. God has made a perfectly balanced planet, and he has told us to take good care of it.

## The Waters Below

Believe it or not, the oceans move around all that weather high in the sky. The oceans hold in heat, keeping our nights warm and our days cool. Like many things in nature, it's all about keeping everything evened out. The earth is constantly trying to even out the temperature in its water and air.

Even though the world is spending lots of time trying to "stay even," it's such a dynamic and exciting place that it will never happen. Heat pours down from the sun and up from inside the earth. As the world turns, the air and water are constantly stirred up. The world is a happening place!

In this never-ending battle to balance the earth's temperature, great rivers of water flow through the oceans, carrying cool water to warm places and warm water to cool places. These currents help to drive "rivers" of air by warming or cooling the atmosphere above the oceans.

WOW! THE OCEAN CAN HOLD A THOUSAND TIMES AS MUCH HEAT AS AIR!

One of the most important currents is called the Gulf Stream. The Gulf Stream is a jet of water that flows across the Atlantic Ocean from the Caribbean up to Great Britain, keeping England warm. The Gulf Stream carries 5,000 times more water than the Mississippi River!

A huge wheel of water turns around the Atlantic, carrying water from Florida up to Canada, across to Europe, down to Africa and back again. It takes many years for this 13,000-mile wheel to turn! The Pacific has a similar ocean river called Kuroshio.

Currents do more than move water around—they move sea life around, too. They carry food from one side of the ocean to another, feeding large schools of fish. Ships use currents to move through oceans faster.

When it gets cold enough, even the ocean freezes! This sea ice is called "pancake ice."

# "Current" Events

In May of 1990, a cargo ship spilled 60,000 sneakers during a storm in the North Pacific. Scientists were able to see where the currents went by following the footwear. Some of the shoes ended up in Oregon, British Columbia, and even Hawaii!

One important current is called El Niño. El Niño is like a moving bathtub of heated seawater that swells or expands across the Pacific Ocean. As the ocean changes, so does the weather above it. Wind patterns shift. Drought comes to places that are normally wet, and dry areas have flooding. Or dry spots get drier and wet ones get wetter. El Niño changes the patterns of weather all over the world. With El Niño, we see one dramatic way that oceans affect the world's climate.

In some places, the ocean is like a giant slushy. Near the north and south poles, the air is so cold that the waters of the sea actually begin to freeze. The sea ice takes on strange forms, first looking like popcorn floating on the waves (this is called frazil ice), and then sticking together into flat frozen "tabletops" and bizarre "pancake" ice.

God's voice thunders in marvelous ways; he does great things beyond our understanding. He says to the snow, "Fall on the earth," and to the rain shower, "Be a mighty downpour..." So that all men he has made may know his work.

Job 37:5-7

The Bible tells us that water came from the sky and from "the springs of the great deep" (Genesis 7:11). Some scientists suggest that part of Earth's water came from comets. Comets are like mountain-sized snowballs in space, and in the beginning of creation, there were zillions of them floating around the newly made solar system. As the comets pelted the earth's atmosphere, they burned up and turned to water vapor. Every day, more water falls to Earth from space as tiny comets! Thirsty anyone?

Huge shelves of ice the size of Colorado stick to the edges of Antarctica and cover the open ocean at the North Pole.

Meteorologists—scientists who study weather—have figured out what causes a lot of God's "signs" in the sky. But just when they think they have it all figured out, God's creation surprises them again.

Weather and climate are very complicated. No matter how much we understand, there's always more to discover. This is one way the creation shows us how wonderful, awesome, powerful, and beautiful the Creator is.

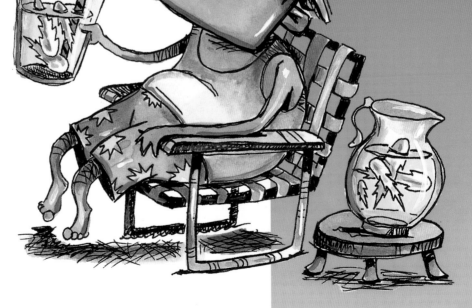

# Forces of Nature or Forces of Creation?

The Old Testament of the Bible was written in Hebrew. In the Hebrew language, there is no word for "nature." Instead, the word "creation" is used. The writers of the Bible knew where nature came from: it was created!

Today, many believe that nature is uncaring and unpredictable. But the people in Bible times saw the world around them as coming from the hand of God. The world was mysterious, yes, but they didn't see its wonderful power as an automatic system. Rather, they saw the creation as the masterpiece of the great artist God.

We see God's power in a thunderstorm, and his grace and beauty in the rainbow that follows. After all, it takes a little rain to make a rainbow! The world is not a giant machine. It is a carefully designed system, crafted by the same craftsman who lovingly made you!

## Setting the Stage for Day Three

As we saw in *Book One* of God's Creation Series, the second day may have lasted for a very long time, or it may have been a normal twenty-four-hour day. However long it was, the oceans and waters above the solid earth were in for a big surprise. Things were happening!

The inside of the earth was restless. Great streams of magma—molten rock—pushed at the sandy floor deep in the ocean. Underwater mountains rose up under the great pressure. On the third day, they would break through the surface of the water, and the first dry land appeared.

Undersea volcanoes rising up also built the dry land. We can see what this process was like off the coast of Hawaii with the undersea volcano called Loihi. Loihi is three thousand feet under the ocean. Wow, that's deep!

It rises from the sea floor in a great cone on the side of the island of Hawaii. From the ocean floor to its summit, Loihi is the height of Mount St. Helens in the state of Washington. Scientists estimate that if Loihi continues erupting, it will become the newest Hawaiian island in a few hundred thousand years.

There are other volcanoes on the ocean floor. In some of the deepest, darkest places, there are hydrothermal vents—volcanic openings where smoke and hot water gushes out. Strange sea life makes its home around many of these vents today. We will see some of these wonderful creatures in *Book Four*.

As volcanoes erupted and magma forced great plains of rock higher and higher, the continents were born. Continental uplift created vast expanses of land that would soon rise above the ocean like gigantic tables of rock.

The continents are made of lighter rock than the heavier stuff deep inside the earth. The continents sit on top of soft, hot rock and move around. Some of this process, called plate tectonics, shoved the edges of continents higher and higher. Eventually they rose out of the ocean.

# The Amazing Disappearing Volcano

In 1979, explorers in a submarine discovered an undersea hydrothermal vent 7,200 feet beneath the surface of the Pacific Ocean. Surrounding this mineral-belching volcano were giant tubeworms and other deep-sea creatures living off nutrients that came from the vent. Scientists called the place "The Rose Garden."

Marine biologists visited The Rose Garden again in 1985, 1988, and 1990, watching how the colony of creatures grew and changed. Then came a surprise! In 2002 scientists visited the vent site again, but it had vanished! Three football fields away, a new vent had erupted, and small versions of the same creatures were living there. This taught scientists that even volcanoes under the sea can be unpredictable!

As the second day comes to a close, we look across the newborn sky. Clouds drift under the sunny heavens, showering the water below with their life-giving rain and snow. Halos ring the sun. Lightning laces the air with the smell of electricity. Waves rise and fall, sloshing around with nothing to crash into. God has lovingly crafted a cradle of life. Very soon, God will cause the dry land to appear, and living things will swim, fly, waddle, and gallop over the whole earth!

# Index

GOD's Creation SERIES

BOOK 1

Space & Time

zonderkidz

Written & Illustrated by Michael & Caroline Carroll
Cartoons by Travis King

IN AUSTRALIA HURRICANES
ARE CALLED WILLY-WILLIES.

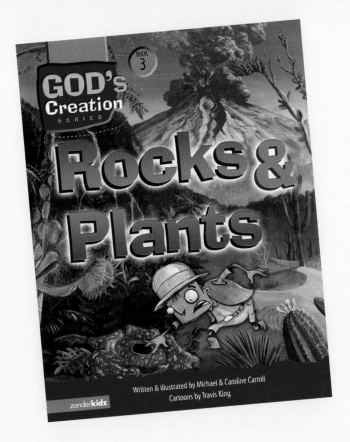

# God's Creation Series
### Written & Illustrated by Michael and Caroline Carroll
### Cartoons by Travis King

Kids will enjoy learning about creation with this set of books—for ages 6 & up

Cartoons, artistic renderings, photographs, fun facts, and more make these informative and entertaining books on creation a rich visual experience— while presenting scientific information.

## Space & Time
**Book 1**
**ISBN: 0-310-70578-9**

## Rocks & Plants
**Book 3**
**ISBN: 0-310-70580-0**

## Sky & Sea
**Book 2**
**ISBN: 0-310-70579-7**

## Fish, Bugs & Birds
**Book 4**
**ISBN: 0-310-70581-9**